Dennis THE MENACE and GNASHER

THE GOLDEN CATAPULT

BY CAVAN SCOTT
WITH ILLUSTRATIONS BY NIGEL PARKINSON

PUFFIN

PUFFIN BOOKS

UK | USA | Canada | Ireland | Australia
India | New Zealand | South Africa

Puffin Books is part of the Penguin Random House group
of companies whose addresses can be found at
global.penguinrandomhouse.com.

puffinbooks.com

Penguin
Random House
UK

First published 2015
001

Printed in China

A CIP catalogue record for this book is available from the
British Library

ISBN: 978–0–141–36213–7

CONTENTS

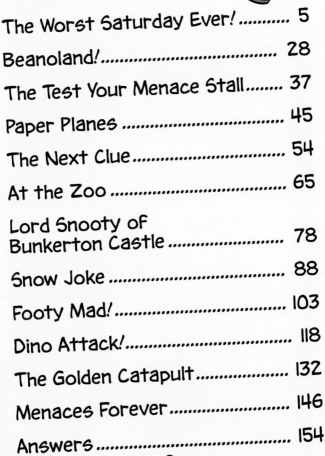

CHAPTER ONE

THE WORST SATURDAY EVER!

'Nooooooooooooooooooooooooooo!'

This was the sound that greeted Beanotown one crisp Saturday morning – a cry of despair so loud you could hear it from the snowy summit of Mount Beano. In fact, you could probably have heard it on the moon.

And who was behind the shout?

It was a boy, but not just any boy.

This was the world's wildest boy.

A boy whose name struck terror into the hearts of parents and teachers everywhere.

A boy who knew more pranks and tricks than anyone else alive.

A boy who owned at least forty-seven identical

red-and-black sweaters. A boy called Dennis the Menace.

Usually, Dennis loved Saturdays. Saturdays meant no school. Saturdays meant hours of causing havoc with his pet Abyssinian wire-haired tripe hound, Gnasher. Saturdays meant fun, fun, fun!

But not today. Today was the worst Saturday ever.

'You can't be serious!' Dennis yelled at

his long-suffering mum. 'A school trip on a Saturday?'

'Don't blame me,' his mum replied, holding out a crumpled note from Bash Street School.

Dear Parents,

We are pleased to announce that we will be taking the children on a trip to the Beanotown Library this Saturday.

The library is hosting a special exhibition of 'Really Old and Quite Dull Books with No Pictures', which I'm sure our pupils will find extremely fascinating.

Please remember that noise is banned in Beanotown Library, as are pea-shooters, catapults, itching powder, sneezing powder, stink bombs, whoopee cushions and water pistols.

Yours sincerely,

Mr De Testa

Headmaster, Bash Street School

'You never know,' Mum added, secretly pleased that someone else would be looking after her, er, darling boy for the day. 'You might enjoy it.'

To her complete and utter surprise, Dennis nodded thoughtfully and said, 'You're right, Mum. Sitting in silence looking at dusty old books sounds like just what I need – especially if it gives me a break from mucking about at the skatepark, BMX-racing or shooting tomatoes at the Colonel's garden-gnome collection.'

Gnasher couldn't believe what he was hearing. Pelting their next-door neighbour's gnomes with squidgy fruit was Dennis's third-favourite pastime. His second-favourite pastime was launching rotten eggs at the Colonel's garden-gnome collection. And his first? Blasting the Colonel's garden-gnome collection into orbit with homemade rockets.

Dennis had planned to do all three today.

But, here he was, Beanotown's Menace of the Year for ten years running, accepting his fate and – worst of all – looking forward to an extra day of school.

'If we're lucky,' Dennis added, 'they might even set us extra homework!'

Dennis's mum fainted from shock.

15

'Can you believe this?' Minnie the Minx asked Dennis, as he scrambled back to his feet. 'It's ruined my plans for a busy day of filling my dad's slippers with custard!'

'That sounds like fun – although cold, lumpy porridge would be better,' said Dennis, who couldn't bear the thought of being out-menaced by the red-haired girl. Everyone else knew that Minnie was just as big a Menace as Dennis, but Dennis would never admit it.

In fact, the Bash Street School bus was filled with all of Beanotown's biggest Menaces!

There was Roger the Dodger, with his checked sweater and trusty dodgePad. Roger always had a scam up his sleeve for getting out of hard work! Then there was Class 2B, also known as The Bash Street Kids. Nine in all, these pesky pupils were in a class of their own when it came to causing chaos.

Together, this busload of bother formed the infamous Menace Squad, and there was no way they wanted to be dragged to a snore-tastic exhibition at the Beanotown Library.

'Don't worry, guys,' said Roger, powering up his dodgePad. 'This calls for Dodge 3128C.'

As the rest of the Menace Squad watched, Roger started tap-tap-tapping away at his screen.

'What are you doing, Rog?' asked Minnie, peering over the Dodger's shoulder.

A wicked smile spread over Roger's face. 'I'm hacking into the driver's satnav,' he replied, the dodgePad beeping wildly. 'Fancy a new destination?'

Immediately the bus swerved to the left. Behind the steering wheel, Class 2B's teacher (known to everyone as simply 'Teacher') struggled to keep up with the changing route.

'Where is this thing taking us?' he said, steering right and then left and then right again.

The kids were thrown gleefully around in the back of the bus as Teacher followed Roger's crazy course.

'Wahoooo!' Dennis whooped, bouncing off the ceiling. 'This is even better than the Vomit Comet roller coaster at Beanoland theme park!'

'Funny you should mention that place,' said Roger, with a knowing grin, before he landed head first on a seat.

But at the back of the bus sat two kids who weren't enjoying the dangerous drive at all.

'Waaaaaah! I want my mumsie!' wailed Walter the Softy, Beanotown's number-one killjoy and Dennis's arch-nemesis. Walter couldn't stand seeing people having fun. When he grew up, he even wanted to become prime minister just so he could ban laughter. What a rotter!

Beside him, Cuthbert Cringeworthy hung on to his seat for dear life. Cuthbert was Class 2B's top swot and a total teacher's pet. Don't think that Cuthbert was as bad as Walter, though. While Walter was a sneaky telltale cheat, all Cuthbert wanted was to be left alone to do his homework. In fact, Cuthbert loved lessons so much that he set himself homework. Extra homework! Imagine that!

'Where are you taking us?' Mrs Creecher squealed from the front of the bus.

'I'm just following the instructions,' Teacher replied, before suddenly slamming on the brakes. 'And here we are!'

The kids were all thrown against the windscreen.

'But where's here?' blubbed Walter, who had landed on Smiffy's head. Not that he had anything to complain about – Smiffy's head was the softest place on the bus!

Dennis peeled himself from the window and stared in amazement when he realized where Roger had brought them.

'Yes!' he shouted, spotting the huge banner just outside the bus. 'We're at Beanoland!'

The rest of the kids scrambled to see. Dennis was right. Roger's new route had brought them to the most amazing, exciting, spectacular and ludicrously dangerous theme park on the planet.

'No!' Mrs Creecher cried, blocking the doors. 'There's no way ANYONE is getting off this bus. We're going to the library and that's final!'

'Oh yeah?' said Minnie, fishing about in her school bag. She pulled out her hand and not one, not two, not even three, but four clockwork mice started running riot around the bus.

'Eeeeeeeeeek!' screamed Teacher, leaping into Mrs Creecher's arms. 'I can't stand mice! I'm scared stiff of the little squeakers!'

This was the chance the Menace Squad had been waiting for. As Mrs Creecher tottered beneath Teacher's weight, the Menaces tore out of the bus. Seconds later, they were racing

towards the Beanoland entrance, cheering at the tops of their voices.

Well, all except 'Erbert, who couldn't see where he was going and ended up running off in completely the wrong direction. Whoops!

'Result!' Dennis shouted as he leapt over the turnstiles. 'Best Saturday ever!'

Which Beanoland attraction does each kid head for, and in which zone of the park? Solve the logic puzzle to find out!

	The Space Zone	The Wild West Zone	The Squelchy Thing Zone	The Spooky Zone	Vomit Comet Roller Coaster	Hall of Mirrors	Test Your Strength Machine	Dodgems
Dennis	X							
Minnie	✓	X	X	X	✓	X	X	X
Roger	X							
Bash Street Kids	X							
Vomit Comet Roller Coaster	✓	X	X	X				
Hall of Mirrors	X							
Test Your Strength Machine	X							
Dodgems	X							

CHEAT!
To give you a helping hand, the first one has already been done for you. Isn't that kind!

FACTS:
1. Minnie rushed straight for the Vomit Comet roller coaster in the Space Zone!
2. Dennis didn't go to the Squelchy Thing Zone!
3. Danny got in trouble when he tripped up a ghost!
4. Roger couldn't wait to go on the dodgems!
5. The Bash Street Kids didn't fancy the Test Your Strength Stall!

〉 Minnie went to the Vomit Comet roller coaster in the Space Zone!

〉 .... went to the ....
in the .... Zone!

〉 .... went to the ....
in the .... Zone!

〉 .... went to the ....
in the .... Zone!

CHAPTER TWO

BEANOLAND!

No one loved Beanoland more than Dennis
the Menace. As well as the twisty-turny Vomit
Comet roller coaster, the theme park had his
all-time favourite fairground attractions. There
was Hook-A-Slug, Splat the Softy and Fling a
Custard Pie at the Policeman. Wahoo!

The only trouble was there was just too
much choice!

'I don't know what to go on first, Gnasher,'
Dennis said as they ran through the theme park.
'What do you fancy?'

As if he had to ask. The wire-haired tripe
hound screeched to a sudden halt and sniffed
the air. 'Gnash! Gnash!' Gnasher barked, before

tearing off to the left.

'Where are you going?' Dennis yelled, struggling to keep up with his pet. When Gnasher picked up a scent, he could run almost as fast as Billy Whizz, the fastest boy in the world.

What has Gnasher smelt? Cross out any letter that appears more than once to find out!

O
Z   N   J   E   T   M
U   F   S
P   T   G   R   P
B   W
L   A
M   J   Z   O   L   F   W   U

Unscramble the remaining letters here:

_ _ _ _ _ _ _ _

29

They raced by both the Coconut Shy and the Coconut Quite Confident stalls, dashed past the Catapult Shooting Gallery and didn't even stop at Gnasher's favourite attraction, Bite the Postie's Bum.

The wonderful whiff hit Dennis as soon as they rushed past the dodgems. Suddenly he knew exactly where Gnasher was heading.

The Beanoland hot-dog seller, who was happily selling his beautiful bangers, had absolutely no idea that a wire-haired tripe hound was charging straight for him – a tripe hound capable of biting through concrete (or really hard Brussels sprouts).

The boy waiting patiently at the front of the hot-dog queue was similarly unaware. This boy was Calamity James, also known as the Unluckiest Boy in the World. James was so unlucky that he hadn't just been struck by lightning once – he'd been struck 983,782 times.

He was so unfortunate that black cats didn't like him crossing their paths.

By James's usual standards, today had actually been quite good. So far, he had only had a piano fall on his head (once), been trampled by a runaway rhino (twice) and discovered that his toilet was full of man-eating piranhas (three times). And that was all before breakfast.

Now, Calamity James was next in line to be served a delicious hot dog. He had his money in his hand and a smile on his face. What could possibly go wrong?

Well, here's a handy step-by-step guide:

Before the hot-dog seller could ask James if he wanted tomato ketchup on his hot dog, Gnasher had leapt up behind the unfortunate lad and landed on his head. **THUD!**

The force pushed James's face down on to the hot-dog counter. **SMACK!**

Before the dazed boy could even look up, Gnasher had chomped his way through all of the sausages. **GNASH! GNASH! GNASH!**

The hot-dog seller was so surprised that he squirted tomato ketchup right into James's eyes. **SQUELCH!**

Unable to see, James bumped into Dennis, who was still chasing after Gnasher. **WALLOP!**

James landed on the floor just as the World-famous Beanoland Hot Dog Stall collapsed . . . on top of him. **CRASH!**

As the dust settled, James's muffled voice could be heard from beneath the wreckage: **'No ketchup for me, thanks!'**

Dennis and Gnasher quickly made a run for it, chased by a furious hot-dog seller.

'Quick, Gnasher,' Dennis panted, pointing to a small gap between the waltzers and a fizzy-pop stall. 'Down here!'

As they ran past the fizzy-pop stall, Dennis snatched a can of cherryade. Giving it a good shake first, he tossed it back over his shoulder like a grenade. The bubbling can bounced once and burst, spraying the hot-dog seller from head to toe in sticky, cherry-flavoured foam.

'Sorry!' Dennis shouted at the spluttering sausage salesman. 'Can't stick around!'

Still laughing, Dennis and Gnasher charged into the next zone of the theme park. 'That was can-tastic, Gnasher! What next?'

The answer was right in front of them.

'Look!' Dennis said excitedly. 'The Test Your Strength machine! How strong do you feel after all those sausages?'

Beside him, Gnasher pulled his best strongman pose. This was enough for the poor Test Your Strength man to quickly decide that it was time for his tea break.

'Awwww!' Dennis groaned when he spotted the CLOSED sign that the stallholder had left swinging on the machine before doing a runner. Gnasher barked in agreement.

'Pssst!' came a voice from behind them. 'What about trying my game?'

Dennis spun round to see a mysterious stallholder standing beside an equally mysterious stall.

'What is it?' Dennis asked, his curiosity getting the better of him.

'See for yourself,' said the mysterious stallholder, throwing a mysterious switch on the side of the mysterious stall.

At once, lights flashed on and tinny fairground music blasted from hidden speakers.

Dennis blinked in the sudden glare, before spotting the revolving targets at the back of the stand. Each target had Walter's face at its centre.

'That's right,' the mysterious stallholder said. 'Step right up for the TEST YOUR MENACE STALL!'

CHAPTER THREE

THE TEST YOUR MENACE STALL

'I'm going to be brilliant at this!' cheered Dennis.

The mysterious stallholder reached into a mysterious sack. 'Then you'd better have this!' he said, producing a shiny green pea-shooter.

'Ha!' Dennis laughed. 'Call that a pea-shooter?' With a swagger, the Menace pulled something from the back of his shorts. '*This* is a pea-shooter!'

Dennis held out his very own patent-pending, self-loading, triple-pea-shooter deluxe.

'I worked on this all summer,' he explained, taking aim. 'But I still haven't had a chance to test it out on Walter. Thanks to your stall, I can get the old Softy over and over and over again!'

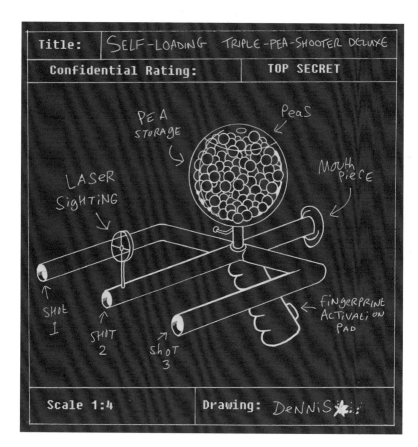

'Help yourself!' the mysterious stallholder said.

Without another word, Dennis put the pea-shooter to his lips and blew.

Rat-a-tat-a-tat-a-tat-a-tat!

One by one, the Softy-faced targets flipped

backwards under the triple-pea-shooter's onslaught. With Gnasher barking happily at his feet, Dennis blasted away until not a single Walter was left.

'Wahoo!' yelled Dennis. 'That was AWESOME!' Then, a thought struck him. 'Hang on! Have I won a prize?'

The mysterious stallholder smiled a mysterious smile. 'Indeed you have, my young Menace. And it is the greatest prize of all!'

Dennis's eyes grew wide. 'Wow! You don't mean as many Slopper-Gnosher-Gut-Bustin' Burgers as I can eat down at Beanotown Burgers?' he asked, his stomach growling at the thought.

'No,' said the mysterious stallholder. 'Much better than that!'

Dennis's eyes grew wider still.

'An all-expenses-paid trip to the anti-gravity skatepark on Mars?' he gasped, ignoring the fact that his dad had repeatedly told him that such a place DEFINITELY did not exist.

'Nope,' said the mysterious stallholder. 'Much, much better than that!'

By this point, Dennis's eyes were the size of dinner plates. 'Hang on! You're not talking about a free pass to be on Santa's Nice List™, no matter how naughty I've been?'

The mysterious stallholder shook his head. 'You'll never guess. It's much, much, much, MUCH better than all of those things put together. It is the ancient and legendary legend of –' here he paused for dramatic effect – 'the Golden Catapult!'

'Woooooooaaaah!' Dennis said, before asking, 'What's the Golden Catapult?'

'What?' the mysterious stallholder scoffed. 'You don't know about the Golden Catapult? And I thought you were supposed to be a Menace!'

Dennis didn't reply, but instead aimed the self-loading triple-pea-shooter deluxe in the mysterious stallholder's general direction.

'F-fine, I'll t-tell you!' stammered the mysterious stallholder. 'The Golden Catapult is an ancient and legendary weapon which only the most menacing can find.'

'Oooooh,' said Dennis.

'Oooooh indeed,' repeated the mysterious stallholder. 'And whoever finds the Golden Catapult will be crowned THE GREATEST MENACE OF ALL TIME!'

'That's me!' Dennis shouted, drawing himself up to his full height. 'I'm the greatest Menace of all time! And, to prove it, I shall find the ancient and legendary Golden Catapult!'

'But what about your friends?' the mysterious stallholder said mysteriously. 'Won't they want to find the Golden Catapult too?'

'Not if I don't tell them about it! The Golden

Catapult will be my secret,' Dennis vowed. 'And my secret alone!'

'Oh yeah?' asked Minnie, who had been standing behind Dennis the whole time, along with Roger and all of The Bash Street Kids.

'You can't have it!' Dennis snapped, spinning on his heel to face the lot of them. 'I'm the greatest Menace of all time!'

'No, I am!' yelled Minnie.

'No, I am!' shouted Roger.

'No, we are!' chorused The Bash Street Kids in unison – except for Smiffy, who shouted 'Happy Christmas!' instead. No one knew why.

Nor did anyone notice the mysterious stallholder laughing mysteriously to himself as they argued.

In fact, Dennis and the rest only realized something was up when the mysterious stallholder mysteriously vanished in a mysterious puff of smoke, along with his mysterious stall and all.

'He was a bit mysterious, wasn't he?' said Roger. 'Where did he go?'

'Perhaps this will tell us!' said Plug, as a piece of paper floated mysteriously down from the air.

'What is it?' asked Toots.

Sidney snatched the paper and turned it over and over in his hands. 'I haven't a clue,' he said, before shrugging and passing the scrap to Dennis.

A grin spread across Dennis's face. 'Yes you have! This is a clue – a clue to the whereabouts of the Golden Catapult!'

'Then what are you waiting for?' asked Minnie. 'Read it to us!'

Dennis's face fell. 'I can't,' he said. 'It's in some sort of code!'

Can you help Dennis to decipher the code and discover the location of the next clue?

T	X	T	C	A	O	U	T	H	N	O	L	I	Y
H	E	C	E	N	F	N	T	E	A	T	N	B	R
E	N	L	U	B	E	D	A	B	E	O	W	R	A

Write the answer here:

_ _ _   _ _ _ _   _ _ _ _   _ _ _

_ _   _ _ _ _ _   _ _

_ _   _ _ _ _ _ _   _ _ _ _   _

CHEAT!
Need help to crack the code?
Then read this message in a mirror!

The letters in the code read downwards
in the first column, upwards in the next
column, down in the next and so on. Get it?
Good!

CHAPTER FOUR

PAPER PLANES

Back on the bus, Mrs Creecher had finally
convinced the still-shaking Teacher to
calm down.

'Right,' she said as they stepped off the bus.
'Now we'd better round up our pupils!'

'You'll be lucky,' said Teacher. 'We'll never get
them out of the theme –'

The two teachers were suddenly trampled by
Dennis, Gnasher, Minnie, Roger and the rest as
they stampeded back on to the bus. The children
raced to their seats, plonked themselves down
and demanded: 'Take us to Beanotown Library
right NOW!'

'One minute they don't want to go, and the

next they can't wait! I'll never understand those kids!' a dishevelled Mrs Creecher moaned as she trudged back aboard the bus.

'Hurry!' Dennis yelled, and the Bash Street School bus sped away from Beanoland.

Five minutes later, the bus pulled up outside Beanotown Library. The Menace Squad didn't even wait for the doors to open. They didn't have to – Fatty just ran straight through the side of the bus, leaving a perfect, Fatty-shaped escape route. The kids streamed out and piled into the library before either of the teachers could stop them.

'So, we know the next clue is in the library,' said Roger. 'But where exactly?'

'Beats me,' said Smiffy, who was standing beside a sign that read: CLUES FOR THE GOLDEN CATAPULT THIS WAY!

'Come on!' shouted Dennis, following the

sign. He tore down a corridor that lead them straight to a large, high-ceilinged room.

'Wait a minute!' said Minnie, stopping on the other side of the big double doors. 'This is where Mrs Creecher was bringing us in the first place!'

'That's right,' agreed Danny, pointing to a poster on the wall. 'It's the exhibition of *Really Old and Quite Dull Books with No Pictures!*'

'Surely the clue can't be somewhere so boring!' said Plug, before a paper aeroplane hit him on the side of the head. 'Hey!' he yelled. 'Who threw that?'

Another paper plane zoomed through the air, this time whacking into Roger. 'Oi!' he shouted. 'Pack it in!'

But the phantom plane-flinger didn't listen. Soon the air was full of paper planes zipping this way and that. The Menace Squad threw their arms above their heads to protect themselves, but just as suddenly as it had begun the flurry of paper planes stopped.

'That was seriously weird,' said Dennis. 'Who throws paper planes in a library, anyway?'

'Er, us?' pointed out Minnie.

'Yeah, but not this time,' said Roger.

'No,' said a voice from behind a bookshelf. 'This time it was me!'

The kids turned to see a mysterious librarian step out of the shadows in what could only be

described as an extremely mysterious way.

'Hey,' said Dennis. 'You're no librarian! You're the mysterious stallholder in disguise!'

'Shhhh,' the mysterious stallholder said, raising a mysterious finger to his mysterious lips. 'Don't tell anyone. Besides, don't you want to know where to find the next clue?'

'Yes,' cried Minnie. 'Tell me – er, I mean, us!'

The mysterious stallholder pointed towards the floor. The kids looked down at the dozens of crumpled paper planes that were lying all over the place.

'One of these planes will lead you to the next clue,' the mysterious stallholder told them. 'But which one?'

With that the mysterious stallholder mysteriously vanished. Again.

'I hate it when he does that,' said Minnie, but Dennis didn't comment. He was too busy searching for the right plane!

Can you find the correct paper plane? It's the one that isn't in a matching pair. Get searching!

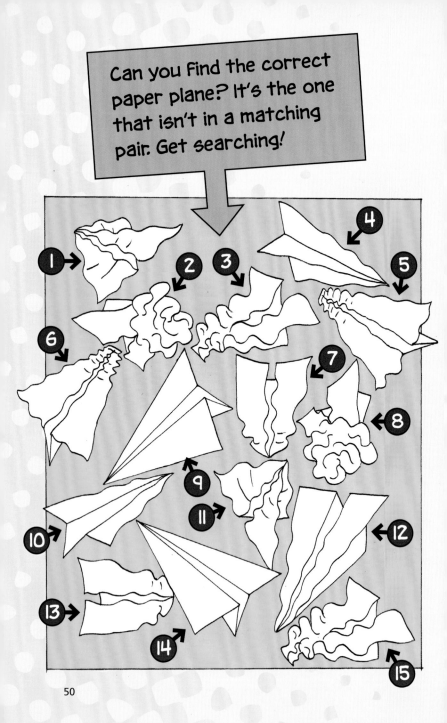

'That's it!' said Dennis, grabbing the paper plane and examining it. 'Huh? It's just blank. There's nothing on it.'

'Your mysterious mate said it would lead us to the clue,' Minnie remembered. 'Why don't you just chuck it and see where it goes?'

'Sounds like a plan to me,' said Roger, snatching the plane from Dennis's hand and throwing it into the air. It twirled and spun and then shot off down between the dusty bookshelves.

'Follow that plane!' shouted Danny, and the Menace Squad did as they were told (for once). When the plane turned left, they turned left. When it turned right, they turned right. And when it soared straight ahead . . . well, you get the idea.

Fatty lead the charge, his feet pounding the wooden floor.

'We need to catch up with him!' Dennis

said, rushing past the others, with Gnasher at his heels.

When he drew close, the Menace whispered in Fatty's ear, 'Hey, Fatty. Have you heard that the library has a new café?'

Fatty immediately started licking his lips. 'A new café? Do they serve doughnuts?'

'Yup!'

'And biscuits?'

'Uh-huh!'

'And cakes covered in cream and cherries and possibly more cakes?'

'Definitely!'

'Wow!' Fatty slurped. 'Where is it?'

'Just turn right at the next bookshelf,' Dennis said with a smirk.

'Thanks, Dennis,' Fatty said, instantly forgetting about the Golden Catapult. 'You're a pal!'

'No problem,' Dennis said, letting Fatty race

on. Still smiling, Dennis spotted the paper plane fly to the left.

But Fatty didn't follow it. He swerved to the right, his thoughts full of doughnuts and biscuits and cake and other gorgeous grub – and the rest of the Menace Squad followed him!

'Haha!' Dennis laughed as he watched them go. 'They think he's still following the plane. Smart or what, Gnasher?'

'Gnesh!' Gnasher barked happily.

'Let's go!' yelled Dennis. 'We don't want them to get their hands on the clue!'

And, with that, Dennis and Gnasher turned left and hurried after the plane.

CHAPTER FIVE

THE NEXT CLUE!

Now alone in the library, Dennis and Gnasher chased after the plane. It darted this way and that, before hitting a large leather-bound book and tumbling to the floor.

'This must be the clue, Gnasher!' shouted Dennis, pulling the heavy book from the shelf. 'Woah! It weighs a ton. But we can't risk looking at it here. The others could be back at any moment.'

Dennis tucked the book under his arm
and ran for the exit. 'Let's get it back to our
tree house!'

Meanwhile, elsewhere in the library, the two
Bash Street teachers were hurrying towards
the *Really Old and Quite Dull Books with No
Pictures* exhibition.

'Mr De Testa will sack us for sure if we lose
the children twice in one day,' Mrs Creecher
complained.

'I know,' fretted Teacher. 'But where can
they be?'

'Watch out! Menace coming through!'
Dennis yelled as he barged past the two adults,
trampling over them in his hurry.

'At least he didn't have that dreadful dog of
his with him,' Mrs Creecher commented just
seconds before Gnasher bounded forward and
landed on her head.

Strange little tiles tumbled from the hollowed-out book and all over Dennis's feet. Spotty bent over and picked one up. 'These are the clue?' he said, peering at the letters on each tile. 'They don't make sense.'

Suddenly Roger realized what they were looking at.

'It's a jigsaw!' he said. 'Quick, someone put it together. I would do it, but I've, er, got a bit of a bad back.'

Rolling their eyes, the rest of the Menace Squad got to work.

Help the Menace Squad to fit the pieces back into the grid! Gnasher has done the first few for you.

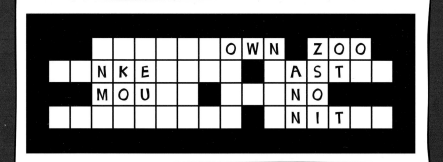

'OK, that's it solved,' said Minnie, once the jigsaw was completed. 'But what does it mean?'

'Each line is a different place in Beanotown,' pointed out Roger. 'Perhaps it means that we have four more clues to find?'

'One in each place?' asked Danny.

'Looks like it,' said Dennis. 'Let's split up. Minnie, you take the first one and then, Roger, you take the next. NO DODGING!'

Roger did his best to look innocent. 'As if I would!' he said, already checking out scams on his dodgePad.

'We'll take the third clue,' Danny offered.

'While me and Gnasher get the fourth,' Dennis said. 'If we work together, we'll find the Golden Catapult in no time!'

'Yeah!' shouted Smiffy, before turning to 'Erbert and asking, 'What's the Golden Catapult?'

CHAPTER SIX

AT THE ZOO

'Yes! There's Beanotown Zoo,' Minnie the Minx said, as she raced towards the gates on her skateboard. 'This is going to be EASY-PEASY!'

But then she skidded to a halt. There was one tiny problem. Beneath the Beanotown Zoo WELCOME sign was a large banner:

WELCOME!

NO MINXES ALLOWED!

'No problem,' Minnie said, kicking off on her skateboard. 'There's an entrance round the back. I'll get in there!'

But, when she got to the back of the zoo, she found yet another enormous banner:

AND THAT MEANS YOU, MINNIE! STAY OUT!

'Pah!' Minnie spat, glaring at the sign. 'I bet this is all because of that time I got the grizzly bears to give me a piggyback. And tied the crocodiles' jaws together with bows. And shaved the gorillas. And went fishing in the shark tank. And taught the bats how to drop water bombs. And gave the penguins rocket packs. And borrowed a tiger to enter in the Beanotown cat show.' Minnie shook her head in disbelief. 'Some people just can't take a joke!'

Now, the one thing you should always remember about Minnie the Minx is that she never gives up! Five minutes later, a tall man in a long raincoat tottered towards the zoo entrance. He wore a hat low on his head, large sunglasses over his eyes and had a big bushy beard.

No one gave him a second glance as he bought a ticket. No one flinched when he stumbled through the turnstile. What no one realized, though, was that this tall, unsteady man wasn't a man at all: he was in fact a small red-haired Minx in disguise. A small red-haired Minx wearing stilts.

'And I'm in!' Minnie yelled in triumph, as the anti-Minx alarms sounded and her false beard fell off. She didn't care. Minnie was up and running before anyone could catch her!

Or so she thought. A hand slapped down on her shoulder, stopping her in her tracks.

'Leggo!' she screeched, but the hand held fast. The hand was connected to an arm, and the arm was connected to a zookeeper.

'Oh, rats!' said Minnie. 'I suppose you're going to chuck me out now, aren't you?'

'Of course not,' said the zookeeper, who suddenly looked mysteriously familiar.

Minnie gasped. The zookeeper was actually the mysterious stallholder from Beanoland in disguise!

'What are you doing here?' Minnie asked.

'I thought you might need some help to find the clue,' the mysterious stallholder said.

'Yes!' Minnie exclaimed, punching the air. 'You rock, Mysterious Stallholder. Go on then. Give me a clue to find the, er, clue!'

The mysterious stallholder tapped the side of his nose and disappeared, leaving only a postcard, which floated down to the ground.

'I really hate it when he does that,' Minnie said, swiping up the card. On one side it had a picture of penguins juggling chainsaws (you'd be amazed at some of the things you can see at Beanotown Zoo), but on the other side there was a riddle written in neat handwriting.

Can you help Minnie solve the riddle-me-ree to find out where the next clue is hidden?

My first is in LIP but not in HIP.
My second is in DING but you won't find it in DONG.
My third is in SON but never in SUN.
My fourth is in NIGHT but not in LIGHT.
My last is in both SING and SONG!

THE CLUE IS IN WITH THE _ _ _ _ _!

'Brilliant!' shouted Minnie, rushing over to the lion enclosure. 'Now I've just got to find a clue inside a cage full of ferocious man-eating beasts! What could be difficult about that?'

She soon changed her mind when she saw the big cats staring at her through the bars – staring at her hungrily.

'Gulp!' she gulped. 'They look more like MIN-eating beasts!'

But she could also see the clue, wrapped up in a little box, with a label that read: PSST! THIS IS THE CLUE!

It was slap bang in the middle of the enclosure.

All I have to do is creep in without them noticing, thought Minnie. 'I know!' she said. 'I'll send them to sleep!'

With that, Minnie snatched a spade from a nearby gardener's shed and tunnelled out of the zoo, under the road to her house and up through her dad's prized petunia patch. Her dad didn't even have time to shout at her. Quick as a flash, Minnie grabbed what she needed from her room and was back down the tunnel before you could say 'Why can't you use a gate like a normal person?'

Back beside the lion enclosure, Minnie sprang

out of the hole with her gear.

'Don't worry,' she told the befuddled beasties. 'I'm just going to send you to sleep with a nice little lullaby.'

She plugged her electric guitar into a stupidly large speaker, turned the volume up to 'ear-splittingly loud' and started to strum!

A lullaby is supposed to lull someone to sleep. That's where the name comes from. It's supposed to be quiet and calming. Minnie's lullaby was not quiet or calming. It was so loud and so hideously out of tune that it upset every single animal in the zoo.

Before Minnie had even reached the end of the first verse, the animals were moaning and groaning and roaring and snorting and braying and honking and squawking.

'Shhhhh!' Minnie hissed at the other animals. 'The lions will never go to sleep with all that racket going on!'

When they refused to settle down, Minnie gave up on the lullaby.

'OK,' Minnie sighed, throwing her guitar over her shoulder (it was caught by a confused baboon). 'Time for Plan B!'

The lions watched as she scrambled down the tunnel. Minutes later, she was back again, lugging Widl carrier bags out of the tunnel's entrance.

Widl is Beanotown's best discount superstore. It's also Beanotown's only discount superstore. You can buy anything in there, which is lucky because Minnie had gone shopping for Antelope-flavoured Extra-chewy Chewing Gum.

'Here you go, lions,' she shouted, chucking the gum into the enclosure. 'Get your gobs around that!'

The lions pounced on the gum and, within seconds, all you could hear was SLOBBER! CHEW! CHEW! SLURP!

'It's worked!' Minnie cheered when the lions' jaws were totally gummed together. 'No teeth means no biting! Now to get the clue!'

Minnie shimmied up the bars and flipped over the top of the cage. She landed metres away from the gummed-up lions and made for the clue.

Unfortunately, Minnie had forgotten that lions don't just have teeth. They also have claws!

The lions swiped at the terrified Minx, who danced around to avoid their huge paws. If she didn't think quickly, she would be mauled to pieces.

Luckily, a Minx is always prepared. Minnie whipped out the water pistol she kept in her sock for emergencies and squirted water at the elephants in the next enclosure.

SPLOSH!

The elephants, who didn't really like their noisy neighbours in the first place, assumed that they'd just been splashed by the lazy lions next door. Miffed, they sucked water up their trunks and blasted it right at the big cats.

SPLURGE!

The lions were drenched in a second, their soggy manes covering their eyes as they coughed and spluttered – which is difficult to do when your jaws have been gummed up with Antelope-flavoured Extra-chewy Chewing Gum.

'Haha!' laughed Minnie, grabbing the wrapped-up box while the wet cats were distracted. 'That'll teach you to menace a Minx.'

Before they could recover, she was up the bars, over the top and back down the tunnel. She'd done it! She had the clue!

Safely in her garden once again, Minnie ripped open the parcel to find two letters.

'Eh? What does that mean?' Minnie asked, as the sound of the chaos she'd caused at the zoo drifted over Beanotown. 'Perhaps it'll make sense when Roger finds his clue. I wonder how he's doing.'

CHAPTER SEVEN

LORD SNOOTY
OF BUNKERTON CASTLE

Roger the Dodger wasn't happy. He'd spent
most of the morning trying to trick other people
into finding the next clue for him, but nothing
had worked.

Grumbling, he had finally given in, and
was trudging towards the majestic towers of
Bunkerton Castle.

'Looking a little down in the mouth there,
young Dodger,' commented a voice, as Roger
stomped through the castle's grounds.

'Who said that?' Roger asked, shocked.

'Only me,' said the owner of the voice. 'Just an
ordinary, mysterious gardener.'

'It's you!' Roger exclaimed as the mysterious stallholder winked at him. This time he was dressed in dirt-covered overalls and leaning on a spade.

'Off to the castle, are you?' the mysterious stallholder said. 'But in which room should you look?'

Roger scratched his head. 'Well, there can't be that many rooms in Bunkerton Castle.'

The mysterious stallholder pulled a Bunkerton Castle visitors' guide from his wheelbarrow. 'It says here there's five hundred and ninety-two rooms. Shouldn't take you long to search them all!'

'Five hundred and ninety-two?' wailed Roger. 'That'll take forever!'

'Then I better leave you another clue,' the mysterious stallholder said, before he vanished, leaving only his spade with a puzzle taped to its handle.

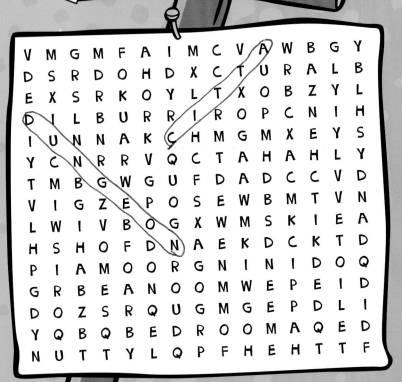

'So, that's where it is,' said Roger as he rushed towards Bunkerton Castle's magnificent front doors. 'But how am I going to get into the armoury?'

Now, most people would probably just ask the owner of Bunkerton Castle if they could look inside the armoury – especially as the owner of Bunkerton Castle is Lord Snooty, the richest boy in the world, and also one of the friendliest.

Unfortunately, Roger never, ever goes for the simple solution. Instead, he's convinced that he has to trick, scam and hoodwink people into doing what he wants. That's why, after consulting his dodgePad, he opted for Dodge 3957F and ran back home to change.

Not long afterwards, Lord Snooty was surprised by a knock on the door.

'I wonder who that is,' the rich kid said,

flinging open the door to reveal a short man wearing an oversized bowler hat, a ridiculous moustache and one of Roger's dad's old suits. As you've probably already guessed, it was actually

Roger in one of his many disguises.

Lord Snooty hadn't guessed, though. In fact, Lord Snooty was completely taken in by the dodge.

'Er, h-hello,' he said nervously. 'Can I help you?'

'Are you the owner of this castle?' asked Roger, bustling into the entrance hall.

'Yes, I am,' replied Lord Snooty.

'Good,' snapped Roger, ticking off an imaginary note on his clipboard. 'Now, I hope you have the appropriate Ghost Licence for this property?'

'A Ghost Licence?' Lord Snooty repeated. 'What's a Ghost Licence?'

'Tsk tsk,' tutted Roger, shaking his head. 'Every haunted castle must have a Ghost Licence. It's either that or pay a one-zillion-pound fine!'

'But Bunkerton Castle isn't haunted,' insisted Lord Snooty.

'I'll be the judge of that!' sneered Roger, before rushing deeper into the castle. 'I need to check every room in the building, starting with the armoury.'

'Check for what?' Lord Snooty asked, chasing after him.

'Ghosts, of course,' said Roger, spotting the armoury door. 'Spirits, spooks, spectres.' He sniggered. 'Heh! I'm the ghost in-spectre!'

Roger didn't wait to see if Snooty laughed at his pun. Instead, he flung open the armoury door.

Inside, he found five suits of shining armour.

'The clue for the Golden Catapult must be in one of these,' he realized. 'But which one?'

Which suit of armour contains the clue? Find the one that's slightly different to the rest!

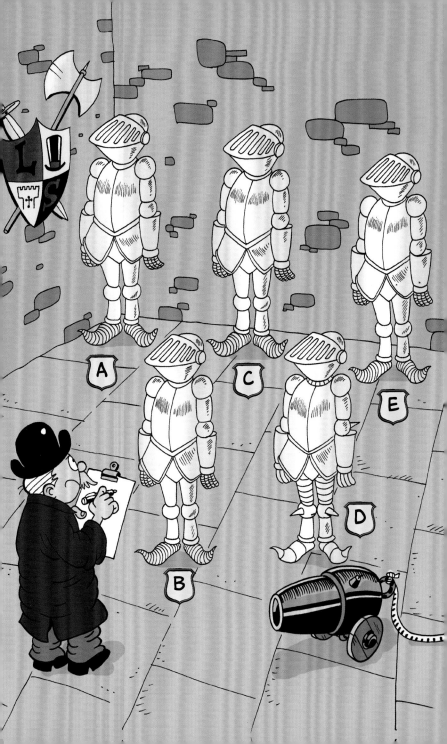

'That's it!' Roger said, rushing to the odd one out. As Lord Snooty puffed into the room, Roger yanked off the helmet and found a small parcel inside.

'It's the clue!' he realized, tearing at the paper. Inside were two letters.

'What does that mean?' he muttered to himself.

'Beats me!' replied one of the suits of armour.

'I haven't the foggiest, either,' said another.

'AAAAAAARGH!' shrieked Roger. 'The castle is haunted! Ruuuuun!'

'Drat!' sighed Lord Snooty. 'I was hoping you wouldn't find out.' He pulled off his top hat and produced a huge wad of money. 'Don't worry – I found a spare zillion pounds down the side of the sofa.'

But Roger didn't stop to swipe the cash. He was too busy running screaming from Bunkerton Castle. In fact, he didn't stop until he was safely hidden beneath his bed at home.

'A-a-a-at least I've g-g-got the c-c-c-clue,' the petrified prankster stammered. 'I h-h-hope The B-B-Bash Street Kids have f-f-found theirs!'

CHAPTER EIGHT

SNOW JOKE

Sadly, The Bash Street Kids were nowhere near finding their clue. In a moment of madness, Danny had asked Smiffy to guide them to the foot of Mount Beano. Instead, Smiffy had guided them to his own foot, which is just as silly as it sounds.

Toots took charge and gave Wilfrid the map to follow. Unfortunately, Wilfrid passed the map to 'Erbert. The short-sighted lad didn't realize that he was reading the map upside-down until they'd started walking to Australia.

It was only when Sidney had the clever idea of taking a cab and charging the fare to Teacher that The Bash Street Kids finally reached Mount Beano's base camp.

'So, where now?' asked Plug, as they scrambled out of the cab.

'Perhaps you should look at that sign over there,' said their mysterious cab driver, before speeding off.

Class 2B stomped over to the sign. They read it. And then read it again. After the third time, they had to admit that they still didn't know what it said.

THN EEXC TLUI EA
ST THT EOO PM
FOUNB TEANO!

'It's gibberish,' said Danny.

'Bless you,' said Smiffy.

'Hang on,' said Toots. 'It's not gibberish – it's another code.'

'But how do we crack this one?' asked Spotty, scratching his head.

Swap the last letter of each word with the first letter of the next. It's as simple as Smiffy when you know how!

THN EEXC TLUI EA ST THT EOO PM FOUNB TEANO!

<u>T h e</u> <u>n e x t</u>

<u>c l u e</u> __ __

___ ____ __

_____ _____!

'What?' said Wilfrid, gazing up at the mountain's snow-topped peak. 'We have to climb all the way up there?'

'Maybe not,' Danny said, spotting something in the distance. 'I've got a brilliant plan . . .'

At the nearby Mount Beano Ski Club, skiers were preparing to use the ski lift to travel up to the summit. Of course, the ski club had a very exclusive membership. School children – especially those from Bash Street – were certainly not allowed to join.

'So how are we going to get in?' whispered Sidney.

Danny pointed to the first-aid hut across the other side of the club. 'See that?'

'Yeah,' replied Fatty. 'But I can't see how it'll help us. We're not sick!'

'No,' grinned Danny. 'But Spotty is about to be!'

'Eh?' said Spotty, not liking the sound of this one bit.

Danny put his arm round his blotchy little friend. 'Guys, it's time for Danny's Brilliant Plan: Part Two!'

Ten minutes later, the skiers were disturbed by a sudden crash from the first-aid hut.

The crash was followed by a low, loud moan.

Then, without any further warning, a small boy staggered out wearing a surgical gown. A small boy covered in spots!

Everyone gasped as two pretty nurses rushed out after the dotty patient. Well, all right – the nurses weren't exactly pretty. They were Plug and Fatty dressed in nurses' uniforms, and it was all part of Danny's brilliant plan!

'Run away, run away!' squealed Plug, doing his best pretty-nurse voice.

'Yes,' agreed Fatty. 'Don't let him touch you!'

'W-why?' the nearest skier asked nervously.

'Because he has snow-zit-itis!' shrieked Plug.

'Snow-whatis?' the skier asked, now even more concerned.

'It's an ultra-rare and mega-contagious condition,' Plug told him.

'And if you catch it,' Fatty continued, 'you'll look just like Spotty in seconds!'

'WAAAAAAAAAAAAAAAAAAAH!' screamed the skiers, running as fast as their ski-booted feet would carry them. 'We don't want to look like that!'

'Cheek!' grumbled Spotty, pulling off his surgical gown as the last skier scarpered.

'Don't worry about them,' Danny yelled, darting towards the ski lift. 'Last one to the top is a bum-face!'

'Oooh, me first!' shouted Fatty, dashing ahead and plonking himself on the ski lift.

Big mistake.

The cables broke with a sharp TWANG, and every pylon crashed down the side of the mountain to land in a heap at the bottom.

'Whoops!' said Fatty.

'Now we're back to square one,' complained Sidney.

'Oooh, are we playing a board game?' asked Smiffy. 'I love climbing up all those snakes and sliding down the ladders!'

'No,' announced Danny, snatching up a discarded ski. 'We're going to ski to the top!'

'Did one of those pylons hit you on the head?' asked Toots. 'You ski down mountains, not up!'

Danny fished his mobile out of his pocket. 'Don't worry! It's all part of Danny's Brilliant Plan: Part Three!'

On the other side of Beanotown, Cuthbert Cringeworthy's phone rang.

'Hello?' he said, picking up the receiver.

'Cuthbert!' yelped Danny on the other end of the line. 'We need your help!'

'My help?' Cuthbert asked, confused. 'Are you sure?'

'Yes!' Danny insisted. 'It's a homework emergency!'

It took Cuthbert precisely 1.972 seconds to dash

all the way to the Mount Beano Ski Club. He really would do anything for homework.

'What's the problem?' Cuthbert panted, completely out of breath. He was so focused on the homework that he didn't notice that the rest of Class 2B were all wearing skis.

'It's dreadful,' said Danny, acting his socks off. 'Teacher has set us extra homework . . .'

'HOORAY!' cheered Cuthbert.

'But he's left it on top of Mount Beano!' Danny continued.

'DISASTER!' wailed Cuthbert. 'Where?'

'Right up there,' Danny said, pointing to the top of the mountain, as the rest of The Bash Street Kids started twirling lassos.

'Never fear,' said Cuthbert, already scrabbling up the side of the mountain. 'I'll save it!'

'Now!' shouted Danny, and the kids let fly with the lassos. They all snagged round Cuthbert, who was climbing faster and faster,

desperate to rescue the
extra homework.
In fact, he was climbing
so fast that he didn't
notice he was dragging
The Bash Street Kids
up the mountain
on their skis.

'This is the way to travel!' whooped Danny, as they zoomed towards the summit. 'Was my plan brilliant or what?'

They reached the snowy peak of Mount Beano in minutes. There, at the very top, was a sign that pointed to neighbouring Dandytown and Nuttytown, but no sign of any homework.

'Where is it? WHERE IS IT?' shrieked Cuthbert, scrabbling around in the snow.

'Oh, yeah. Well, about that . . .' Danny began. He was about to explain his small fib when Cuthbert froze. Something had happened. Something a bit odd!

Can you help Smiffy put the pictures in the right order to show what happened next?

99

'Wahey! Well done, Plug!' shouted Danny. 'You scared that hairy old yeti silly!'

'I don't understand how.' Plug shrugged. 'It only looked at my face!'

'Exactly,' laughed Toots.

Beneath their feet, the snow started to shake as the ground rumbled.

'Is that your stomach again, Fatty?' Spotty asked.

'Not me,' said Fatty, tucking into a post-lunch, pre-dinner, family-sized bag of chocolate-cake-flavoured crisps.

The shaking got worse!

And worse!

AND WORSE!

'It's the yeti's scream!' shouted Sidney, as the snow from the summit began to slide down the side of the mountain. 'It's started an avalanche!'

'Then it's a good job we're still wearing skis!' Danny shouted. 'Let's go!'

Together, The Bash Street Kids skied down
the side of the mountain ahead of the avalanche,
whooping and laughing all the way until they
slid to a stop back at the base camp.

'Hang on,' said 'Erbert, as they came to a rest
at the bottom. 'What about the clue?'

'No!' said Danny, slapping a hand over his face. 'We forgot to look for it!'

'Look for what?' said Smiffy, running up to join his friends and carrying a parcel wrapped in bright paper.

'That must be the clue,' said Danny. 'Where did you find it?'

'At the top of the mountain,' Smiffy said. 'Is it important?'

Danny snatched the parcel and ripped it open. Inside were two letters.

'Good work, Smiffy!' said Danny, holding the clue up in triumph. 'We did it!'

'Yeah,' said Toots. 'I hope Dennis has been as lucky!'

CHAPTER NINE

FOOTY MAD!

Cold Trafford, the Beanotown United stadium, was already buzzing when Dennis and Gnasher arrived outside. The fans were singing, the teams were warming up and penguins were juggling chainsaws in the car park (well, they fancied a break from the zoo!).

'Here we are, Gnasher,' said Dennis. 'But where is the clue? Cold Trafford is massive!'

Gnasher was about to shrug, when a nearby pie seller waved them over to his stall. A familiar, mysterious pie seller.

'It's you!' Dennis said, as he ran over to the mysterious stallholder. 'Are you here to help me find the clue?'

'Nah,' said the mysterious stallholder. 'I'm here to sell pies. Do you want one?'

'What's in them?' asked Dennis, sniffing the pastry suspiciously.

'It's a mystery,' the mysterious stallholder said in his most mysterious voice yet.

'Fair enough,' said Dennis, flipping the stallholder a coin and pointing to the biggest pie of them all. 'I'll have that one!'

'A good choice, my young Menace,' said the stallholder, passing Dennis the large, steaming pie. 'I hope its contents won't be too much of a puzzle!'

Dennis frowned. 'You're going to mysteriously vanish now, aren't you?'

The mysterious stallholder looked hurt. 'What makes you think that?' he asked, before pointing over Dennis's shoulder and saying, 'Oh, look! A young girl shaving a gorilla!'

'Where?' Dennis said, glancing over his

shoulder, but when he looked back the man was gone and so were all the pies.

'Ah well,' Dennis said, holding up the pie that the stallholder had given him. 'Mum always says you shouldn't search for cryptic clues to the location of an ancient and legendary weapon on an empty stomach anyway.'

As Gnasher licked his lips, Dennis took a big bite of the pastry.

CHOMP!

'Ugh,' he groaned. 'This pie is filled with paper!'

Throwing the pastry to the ground (where it was swiftly gnoshed by Gnasher), Dennis unravelled the paper filling.

'Hang on,' he said. 'He wasn't joking about the contents of the pie being a puzzle! Look!'

Dennis held the paper up to Gnasher. It was covered in a baffling brainteaser.

Can you fit all the footy words into the grid? Dennis has started it for you!

FOUR LETTERS
CLUB
FOUL
KICK
PASS
TEAM

SEVEN LETTERS
PENALTY
PLAYERS
STRIKER
~~WHISTLE~~

FIVE LETTERS
MATCH
PITCH

NINE LETTERS
GOALPOSTS

Unscramble the letters in the yellow boxes to find where the next clue is hidden!

The next clue is in the: — — — —

'That's it!' cheered Dennis. 'Quick, let's get into the stadium!'

Dennis and Gnasher vaulted the turnstiles and dodged the stewards before dashing into the stands. On the pitch, the ref blew his whistle and the game began.

'Oh no!' Dennis said. 'We've missed kick-off! How are we going to get the ball while it's on the pitch?'

Out of the corner of his eye, Dennis spotted a large fuzzy bear heading towards the players' tunnel.

'Of course,' he said, snapping his fingers. 'We need to get into the game. This way, Gnasher!'

Nearby, in the changing rooms, the bear took off his head. This wasn't as gross as it sounds, as the bear was actually Beanotown United's official mascot. Beneath the costume was Postie, Beanotown's very own postman.

The bear suit was hot and sticky, and the hairs got up his nose, but Postie didn't care. Today was his day off, and he loved playing the Beanotown United mascot for one reason and one reason alone: Gnasher was nowhere near him!

From Monday to Friday, Dennis's dog menaced poor Postie. He barked at Postie. He snarled at Postie. He chased Postie. And he even chewed Postie.

Yes, biting postmen's bums was right up there with wolfing down sausages and burying bones when it came to Gnasher having fun. Was it any wonder that Postie was normally so nervous? Not today though.

Postie sighed happily as he reached for a water bottle. 'This costume may be boiling,' he said, having a drink, 'but at least that dog is nowhere to be seen!'

113

115

Soon, the rest of the Menace Squad was gathered in Dennis's tree house.

Minnie was the last to arrive, proudly waving the letters she'd found. 'I got my clue!' she declared happily.

'Me too!' said Roger, still shaking slightly from his spooky encounter.

'And so did we,' said Danny, brushing snow from his cap.

'Fantastic!' cheered Dennis, producing his own clues from his pocket. These ones read:

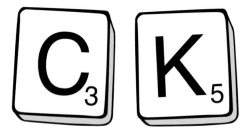

'But what do they all mean?' asked Plug, scratching his head.

CHAPTER TEN

DINO ATTACK!

There are lots of odd things in Beanotown. There are secret caves under Bash Street School, mutant rats in the sewers, a secret time machine in the clock tower and even a fruit-powered superhero called Bananaman.

But nothing is as odd or weird or strange or downright creepy as the island in the middle of the duck pond. Imagine every nightmare you've ever had and multiply it by one billion: that's how scary it is.

Of course, Minnie didn't find it scary at all. 'I don't think it's scary at all,' she said, to prove it.

The Menace Squad stood on the banks of the duck pond, looking across at the island with its smouldering volcano and tall tropical trees. No one really understood how that lot could even fit on such a small island in the first place. It really was a magical place. From a distance it looked tiny, but up close it was massive.

'So how do we get over there?' asked Plug.

'With this!' announced Roger, pulling a little rubber ball from his pocket.

'Oooh, what is it?' asked Toots.

Roger chucked the ball into the air, where it immediately started to swell up.

'My Emergency Inflatable Dodge Dinghy,' Roger replied smugly, as the now fully inflated boat slapped back down beside them. 'Never leave home without it. All aboard!'

The Menace Squad scrambled into the dinghy. There was only one problem: the boat was still on dry land!

'Er, how do we move?' asked Sidney. 'There aren't any sails or oars or anything.'

'Not a problem,' said Roger, pulling a large plate from his pocket. On the plate was a big, steaming sausage.

'What's that?' asked Wilfrid.

'Only my Emergency Dodge Banger with Extra Onions!' said Roger. 'I always have one handy in case I have to bribe Gnasher.'

He turned to the dog, whose mouth was already watering wildly. Roger pulled the plate away from him. 'No, Gnasher. You can only have the sausage if you swim across to the island, pulling the boat behind you.'

Gnasher looked at the sausage, and looked at the duck pond. Then, thinking that swimming was too much like having a bath, Gnasher jumped up and gnashed the Emergency Dodge Banger, the extra onions and the plate anyway.

'Waaaah! My hand!' wailed Roger, blowing on his nibbled fingers, while the rest of the Menace Squad groaned.

'Now we'll never get across to the island,' whined Fatty, who was secretly annoyed that he hadn't got to scoff the juicy sausage himself.

'If you need something done, get a Minx to do it,' snapped Minnie, pulling a pin out of her pocket.

'No, Minnie! Wait!' yelled Spotty, but it was too late. Minnie pushed the pin into the side of the inflatable dinghy.

POP!

The boat took off like a rocket, thrown forwards by the escaping air.

'AAAAAAAAAAARGH!' yelled the Menace Squad, as they soared up and swooped down, looped several loops and landed in the middle of Duck Pond Island.

CRUMP!

'That was brilliant!' yelled Minnie, jumping from the deflated dinghy as her dazed, dizzy friends staggered from the wreckage. 'Can we do it again?'

'NO!' they all replied.

'OK, we're here,' said Dennis, his eyes still spinning. 'So, what next?'

'Perhaps we get attacked by that giant green Tyrannosaurus rex?' suggested Smiffy.

'Don't be daft, Smiffy,' said Danny, before they were all attacked by the giant green Tyrannosaurus rex.

'ROOOOOOAR!' roared the dinosaur.

'SCREEEEAM!' screamed the kids.

'Oooooh, can we keep it as a pet?' asked Smiffy.

Dennis hauled Smiffy out of the way of the T-rex's snapping jaws. 'Hide!' he shouted.

The Menace Squad froze behind a large rock, hardly daring to move.

On the other side of the rock, the T-rex stomped up and down, sniffing the air.

'What's it doing?' asked 'Erbert.

Somewhere in the back of Dennis's mind, something happened. Something that had never happened before. Dennis remembered something useful he'd learned at school.

'T-rexes have rubbish eyesight,' Dennis said. 'Even worse than 'Erbert's!'

'Oi! I heard that, Dennis,' said 'Erbert, waggling his finger at Minnie.

'But they do have a brilliant sense of smell. It's trying to sniff us out!' Dennis said.

'Then let's give it a reek to remember,' said Fatty, shrugging off the backpack he'd been carrying ever since they'd left the tree house.

'What's in there?' asked Plug, as Fatty started to rummage around in the bag.

'This!' Fatty said, pulling out a large tin can.

'Windy Beans?' Minnie said, peering at the label.

Fatty pulled out three more cans and started sharing them around.

'I thought I – er, I mean, we might get hungry. Don't worry. There's enough for everyone.'

Soon every member of the squad had a can of Windy Beans in their hands.

'OK, everyone,' said Fatty. 'Tuck in!'

Together, they pulled open their tins and poured the cold beans down their throats.

Now, Windy Beans are just like the baked beans you probably enjoy on toast. And, just like baked beans, if you eat too many, they can cause your bum to make naughty noises and nasty niffs. The difference with Windy Beans, though, is that they are roughly one billion times more powerful.

The moment the Menace Squad had finished scoffing the beans, their stomachs started rumbling. Something was brewing in their bellies. Something dreadful.

'Oooh, my tummy feels funny!' said Toots, clutching her middle.

'Don't hold it in!' said Dennis, grabbing on to the rock just in case he blew himself into the air.

'Let 'em rip!' shouted Fatty.

And, with that, the Menace Squad dropped the most powerful, most pungent series of parps in the history of pumping! It was louder than a thousand elephants singing the national anthem and smellier than any cheek-squeak ever trumped. If there was a World Record for the Greatest Guff of All Time then this blow-out would have broken it without question!

The unfortunate T-rex got the full blast of the botty-burp barrage right between the nostrils.

PHAAAAAAAAAAAAAAAAAAARTT!

THUD!

That thud, in case you were wondering, was the sound of a nine-ton T-rex collapsing after being gassed by a bunch of ten-year-old school kids.

'Wahey!' shouted Dennis, jumping on top of the rock. 'Well done, Fatty. We knocked it out cold!'

'Well done indeed,' said a mysterious voice as a mysterious explorer stepped mysteriously out from behind a humongous fern.

The mysterious stallholder greeted the Menace Squad as if they were old friends, throwing his spindly arms out wide.

'Congratulations, my young youths! You have passed all the tests. You followed the clues, you crossed the duck pond and you even gassed a ferocious dinosaur. You truly are worthy of the Golden Catapult!'

'What?' asked Dennis. 'All of us?'

'Yesssss,' hissed the mysterious stallholder. 'Now you just need to dig it up!'

Suddenly, as if by magic, a scroll appeared in his hand. The mysterious stallholder threw it to Smiffy, who failed spectacularly at catching it. Luckily, it bounced off his head and landed in Dennis's hands.

The Menace unrolled the paper to reveal a faded map.

'It's Duck Pond Island,' he gasped.

'That it be,' said the mysterious stallholder who, oddly, was now wearing a pirate hat and eyepatch. 'And X marks the spot where the treasure be buried, that it does. Arrrrr!'

Dennis gave the mysterious stallholder a withering look. 'First,' he said, 'you're not a pirate, mysterious or otherwise. And second, there's no X on this map!'

The mysterious stallholder looked over Dennis's shoulder and scratched the back of his mysterious neck. 'Oh yeah, you're right. I must have forgotten to draw it on.' He shrugged. 'Never mind! There are co-ordinates on the back. Follow them and you'll find the Golden Catapult. It's not as dramatic, but beggars can't be choosers, can they?'

Yaaaarrrrr-har-de-har-haaaaar, ye scurvy swabs! Follow the co-ordinates on yer map to find where the Golden Catapult be buried, ye lily-livered bilge-bags! Savvy?

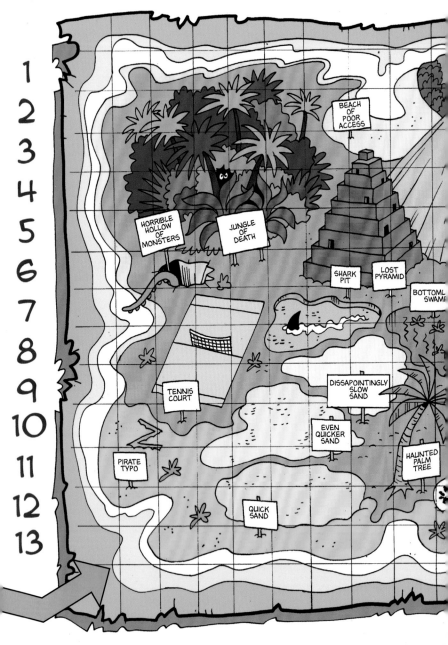

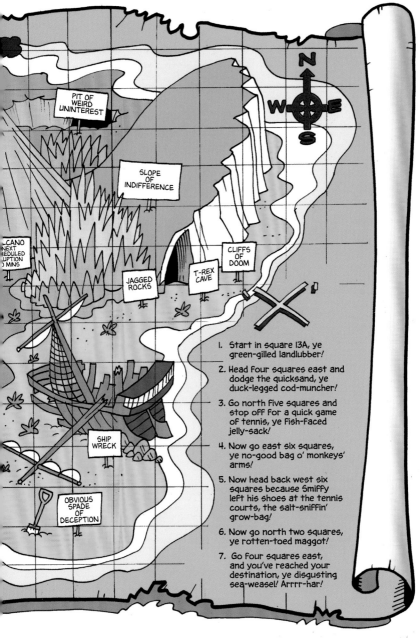

CHAPTER ELEVEN

THE GOLDEN CATAPULT

'That's got to be it!' said Dennis, pointing at the map. 'Right next to the lost pyramid.'

'How can it be a lost pyramid if we know where it is?' asked Roger.

'Who cares?' yelled Minnie, setting off at a run. 'Let's get digging!'

The Menace Squad followed the map's instructions, darting this way and that. They passed weird tombs dating back thousands of years, bizarre flightless snails and even a totem pole that looked exactly like Plug's mum.

Finally, they reached the end of the trail, and found a huge X painted on the ground.

'Oh, I knew I put it somewhere,' remembered

the mysterious stallholder, shaking his head and chuckling.

This time Dennis didn't bother giving a withering look. He rushed straight over to the pile of tools that someone had conveniently left next to the big X.

'It's OK,' he said, brandishing a shovel. 'I've got a treasure-digger-upper!'

'Why can't you just call a spade a spade?' Danny said. He snatched the shovel from Dennis's hands and started digging. The other kids joined in – although none of them could dig as well as Gnasher, who was soon covering the mysterious stallholder in flying soil.

'Don't mind me! Cough!' hacked the mysterious stallholder, as the Menace Squad dug deeper and deeper and deeper and – you guessed it – deeper still.

Then, finally, Dennis's spade hit something very hard.

CLUNK!

'It's a chest!' he cried. 'Quick! Help me get it out of the hole!'

Together, Dennis, Minnie, Roger and the rest hauled and heaved the battered wooden chest up to the top of the hole.

'Look,' said Roger, rattling a large padlock on the dirt-covered lid. 'It's locked. And we haven't got a key.'

'Who needs a key?' asked Dennis, winking at Gnasher. 'Eh, boy?'

Gnasher gave one happy bark then bit the lock in two.

GNASH!

The lid of the chest flipped open and
the Menace Squad was bathed in an eerie
golden light.

Dennis leaned into the chest and switched off
the light.

'There. I can see now,' he said, rubbing his eyes.

'But what can you see?' asked the
mysterious stallholder.

'This!' declared Dennis, pulling a catapult
from the bottom of the chest. But not just any
old catapult. Oh no. This was . . .

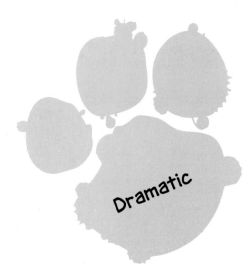

Dramatic

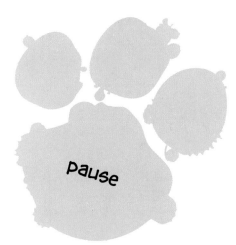

pause

. . . THE GOLDEN CATAPULT!

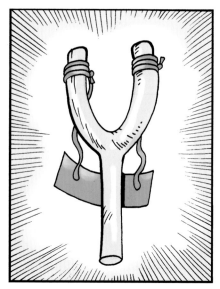

'It's mine!' Dennis laughed. 'I'm the greatest Menace of all time!'

'You're joking, aren't you?' spluttered Minnie, making a grab for the catapult. 'Give that to me, toilet-brush hair!'

'Hey, I'm the biggest Menace,' yelled Roger, trying to pull Minnie's hands away.

'No, I am!' shouted Danny, pushing the others out of his way.

Soon, the other kids had all joined in the argument.

'No, I'm a bigger Menace that you are!'

'No, I am!'

'I am!'

'I am!'

'I am!'

'I am!'

'I am!'

'I'm not!'

OK, that last one was Smiffy, but you get the idea.

Before long, the kids were fighting, scrapping, shoving, kicking and doing all kinds of other naughty stuff.

They were so busy they didn't notice a mysterious hand reach into the punch-up and pinch the Golden Catapult from Dennis's grasp.

'Hey! Who took that?' Dennis cried out, realizing just a moment too late it was gone.

'ME!' crowed the mysterious stallholder, holding the Golden Catapult above his head like a trophy. 'My plan has worked perfectly!'

'Your what?' asked Minnie.

'My perfectly cunning and delightfully devious plan,' said the stallholder. And then he started to pull off his own face.

'Ugh!' said Roger. 'That's disgusting, even for us!'

'It's just a mask, you fool,' scoffed the stallholder, as he finally removed his disguise and revealed his true identity to the world.

'WALTER?!' Dennis gasped.

Yes, standing in front of them was Walter, Dennis's arch-nemesis and King of the Softies!

'It was you all the time?' Dennis spluttered in disbelief. 'You gave us the clues? You helped us find the Golden Catapult?'

'You found it for me!' Walter jeered. 'Only a true Menace could find the catapult – and, in tricking you, I've proved that I am the greatest Menace of all time! AND I CLAIM MY PRIZE!'

Light erupted from the catapult, a glow brighter than the sun. The Menace Squad had to look away, and when they looked back . . .

'No!' Dennis cried out. 'You're wearing red-and-black stripes!'

It was true. Walter's sweater was red and black, topped by a small red-and-black bow tie!

'This can't be happening,' said Minnie.

'Oh, but it is!' Walter sneered. 'And, if I'm a Menace, that must make you SOFTIES!'

'Stop him!' shouted Dennis, but it was too late. Wave after wave of golden energy blasted out from the catapult, bending everything to Walter's will.

When the glow finally faded, Beanotown was transformed into Softytown, the dullest, unfunniest place on the planet.

But that wasn't the worst of it.

Dennis looked around slowly at his friends. He couldn't believe his eyes. They all looked so . . . neat and tidy.

Roger was wearing a sensible cardigan (complete with bow tie), Minnie was wearing a pretty pink dress, and The Bash Street Kids were all in crisp, clean school uniforms.

Then Dennis's eyes settled on Gnasher, who – horror of horrors! – was now a fluffy white poodle.

In Gnasher's sad eyes, Dennis spotted his own reflection.

The shirt.

The tie.

The long trousers.

The slicked-back, neatly parted hair.

'You've gone too far this time, Walter!' Dennis snapped, turning on his nemesis. 'You can't do this to us!'

'Oh I can, and I have!' chuckled Walter. 'From this day on, you'll never pull another prank or laugh at another joke! Your menacing days are OVER!'

'But what will we do?' Minnie sniffed, curling her cute new ringlets round her finger.

'Oh, don't worry!' jeered Walter. 'I've got some lovely new hobbies for you all!'

144

Dusting!

Extra homework!

Dolls' tea parties!

Collecting ancient Roman shopping lists!

CHAPTER TWELVE

MENACES FOREVER

Walter clapped delightedly when he saw the
Softified Menaces forced to do the things they
hated most of all.

'Oh, we're all going to be such friends,' he
said, grinning from ear to ear. 'And, after you've
finished all this, how's about we go and watch
some paint dry? You'll love it. It's no fun at all!'

'Urrrrgggh,' groaned the Menaces, all at the
same time.

'If only my pal Mrs Creecher could see you all
now,' Walter chuckled, undoubtedly to rub it in.

The Menace Squad couldn't believe this was
happening to them. Maybe it was the worst
Saturday ever after all!

'I don't believe it,' Walter sobbed. 'All my plans, ruined!'

Above him, the Menace Squad cheered and clapped and fist-pumped, happy to be back the way they should be: Menaces and proud!

'We don't need ancient and legendary stuff to be the world's greatest Menaces,' Dennis said.

'Yeah,' Minnie agreed. 'It's in our blood!'

'Especially when we work together,' Roger added.

Walter pounded his fists into the ground. 'I knew it was a mistake to send you after the Golden Catapult! I should have tried to trick you into finding the Golden Whoopee Cushion instead!'

'Wait a minute,' said Danny, his mouth dropping open. 'There's a Golden Whoopee Cushion?'

'Ooooh,' said Minnie. 'I bet only a real Minx can find that!'

'What are you talking about?' cut in Roger. 'It sounds like a job for a Dodger to me!'

'Don't be stupid!' Dennis laughed. 'What you need is the biggest Menace in history: me!'

And, with that, the Menace Squad raced off, already arguing about which of them was going to find the Golden Whoopee Cushion first.

Well, you know what they say . . .

Some Menaces never learn!

THE END!*

*Just in case you hadn't worked that out already.

ANSWERS

Pages 26-7

	The Space Zone	The Wild West Zone	The Squelchy Thing Zone	The Spooky Zone	Vomit Comet Roller Coaster	Hall of Mirrors	Test Your Strength Machine	Dodgems
Dennis	✗	✓	✗	✗	✗	✗	✓	✗
Minnie	✓	✗	✗	✗	✓	✗	✗	✗
Roger	✗	✗	✓	✗	✗	✗	✗	✓
Bash Street Kids	✗	✗	✗	✓	✗	✓	✗	✗
Vomit Comet Roller Coaster	✓	✗	✗	✗				
Hall of Mirrors	✗	✗	✗	✓				
Test Your Strength Machine	✗	✓	✗	✗				
Dodgems	✗	✗	✓	✗				

> MINNIE went to the VOMIT COMET ROLLER COASTER in the SPACE Zone!

> DENNIS went to the TEST YOUR STRENGTH MACHINE in the WILD WEST Zone!

> ROGER went to the DODGEMS in the SQUELCHY THING Zone!

> THE BASH STREET KIDS went to the HALL OF MIRRORS in the SPOOKY Zone!

Page 29
Gnasher can smell BANGERS.

Page 44
The next clue can be found at the BEANOTOWN LIBRARY.

Page 50
The odd one out is plane number 14.

Page 63

Page 70

My First is in LIP but not in HIP.
My second is in DING but you won't find it in DONG.
My third is in SON but never in SUN.
My Fourth is in NIGHT but not in LIGHT.
My last is in both SING and SONG!

THE CLUE IS IN WITH THE **LIONS!**

Page 80
The missing word is ARMOURY.

VERY HEAVY WEIGHT INDEED

```
V M G M F A I M C V A W B G Y
D S R D O H D X C T U R A L B
E X S R K O Y L T X O B Z Y L H
D I L B U R R I R O P C N I Y S
I U N N A K C H M G M X E H Y S Y
Y C N R R V Q C T A H A H C V D
T M B G W G U F D A D C C T V N A
V I G Z E P O S E W B M I E D A
L W I V B O G X W M S K I T O A D
H S H O F D N A E K D C K O I Q
P I A M O O R G N I N I D I L D
G R B E A N O O M W E P E L I D
D O Z S R Q U G M G E P D E I D
Y Q B Q B E D R O O M A Q T D F
N U T T Y L Q P F H E H T F
```

Page 85
The odd suit of armour is D.

Page 90
The next clue is at the
top of Mount Beano!

156

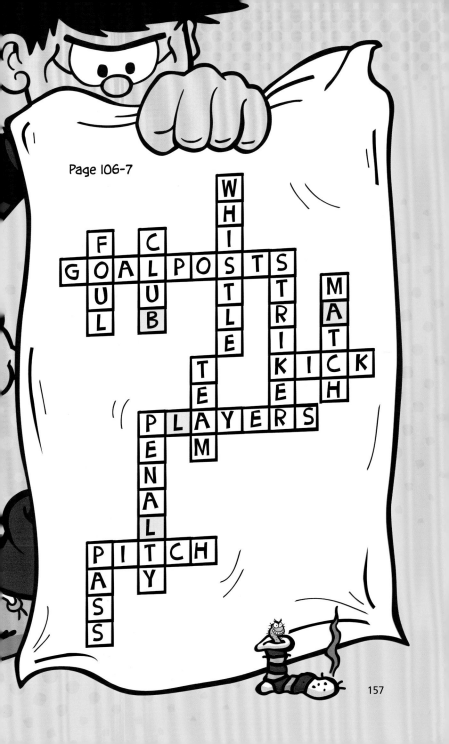

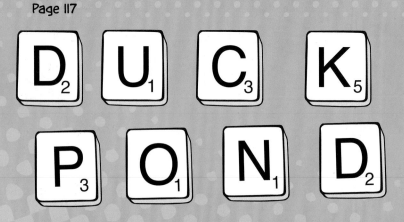

DUCK POND

Page 130-1
The Golden Catapult is in square 61, by the Lost Pyramid.

Page 144
Dennis: COLLECTING ANCIENT ROMAN SHOPPING LISTS!
Minnie: DOLLS' TEA PARTIES!
Roger: DUSTING!
The Bash Street Kids: EXTRA HOMEWORK!

WHY NOT MAKE YOUR OWN MENACE JOURNAL?

THE Diary of
Dennis
THE MENACE

MENACE IT
Yourself!
SCRIBBLE JOURNAL

I've menaced my diary . . . now it's time to menace yours!

Join *The Beano* comic's front-page legend as he guides
you through everything you need to know to create a book
just like his. Your teacher will hate it!

KIDS RULE IN BEANOTOWN!

WANT MORE DENNIS THE MENACE?

JOIN HIM EVERY WEDNESDAY IN . . .

www.beano.com